CW00840389

The Old Man
and the
Turnip

Illustrated by Maureen Bradley

AWARD PUBLICATIONS LIMITED

ISBN 0-86163-958-8

This edition copyright © 1999 Award Publications Limited

First published 1999
Second impression 2000

Published by Award Publications Limited,
27 Longford Street, London NW1 3DZ

Printed in Singapore

Once there was a poor old farmer who lived in a little village in the mountains. All summer he worked in his garden to raise enough vegetables for the long winter. So busy was he from morn till night that his good wife scarcely ever saw him.

At length the time of year came for the harvest to be gathered. The Mayor of the village called all the farmers together and offered a handsome award for the largest turnip to be harvested. The award was to be a most desirable black-spotted cow.

Now the old Farmer had no cow, and he said to himself, "With a cow we would have cheese to offer all who passed our way. What a fine thing that would be!"

So saying, and thinking how elegant the black-spotted cow would look in his barn, he trudged home and fell to work harder than ever.

Before long all but the last row of turnips had been laid away for the winter. But the full storehouse gave the Farmer no joy, for his mind was full of the beautiful black-spotted cow, and his turnips were of no great size.

"Alas," said he, "there is nothing here to win an award!"

Hardly had the words left his mouth when a strange thing happened. He came upon a turnip which would not move with his pulling. Taking a better hold, he pulled and pulled, but still the turnip would not move from the ground.

In great excitement he made his way across the fields to the little stream where his wife was scouring the pans.

"Good woman, Good woman," he shouted. "Come and help me! I have found a turnip so large that I cannot pull it from the ground single-handed."

So the Farmer's Wife dropped her pots and pans and hurried after the Farmer. Together they pulled and tugged, and tugged and pulled, but the turnip would not come up.

At length she said, "It is plain to be seen that this turnip is too much for two such old people. I will run and fetch our grandson. He is young and strong."

So she searched down the lane till she saw the Grandson bringing home the geese.

"Come quickly," she shouted. "We have found a remarkable turnip and cannot pull it up without your help!"

Leaving the geese to get home by themselves, the Grandson hurried to the place where the turnip grew.

Then the Farmer grasped the turnip, the Farmer's Wife held fast to the Farmer, and the Grandson held fast to the Farmer's Wife.

All three pulled and tugged, and they tugged and pulled.

Finally the old woman said, "Alas, this turnip is too strong for three. Run and fetch our granddaughter!"

So the Grandson ran to
summon the Granddaughter,
and found her watching the
sheep and knitting.

"Leave the sheep and come at
once," shouted the Grandson.
"There is a big turnip which
three of us cannot pull from
the ground!"

Dropping her knitting in her
haste, the Granddaughter flew
to the field where the turnip
grew.

Again the Farmer took hold
of the turnip, the Farmer's Wife
took hold of the Farmer, the
Grandson took hold of the
Farmer's Wife, and the Granddaughter took hold of the
Grandson. Together they pulled
and tugged, and tugged and
pulled, but still the stubborn
turnip remained in the ground.

"Enough of this," said the
Farmer's Wife. "We must have
more help. Run and fetch our
neighbour!"

So the Granddaughter ran to the next farm, where she found the Neighbour pouring herself a cup of coffee.

"Lose no time but come and help us," shouted the Granddaughter, "for we have found the largest turnip in the world!"

So the startled Neighbour dropped her cup of coffee and hurried off to join the others in the turnip field.

"Surely with five pulling, the turnip must come up," said the Farmer's Wife.

But when the Farmer, the
Farmer's Wife, the Grandson,
the Granddaughter, and the
Neighbour had pulled and
tugged in vain, the good
Neighbour said, "What is
needed here is a strong man."

And off she went to call the
Milkman.

Soon she met him coming down the road from milking.

"What big news!" she exclaimed. "The Farmer has found a turnip so large that five people cannot pull it up. Come and help us, for there is none so strong as you in the whole village!"

Pleased with this flattery, the Milkman left his pails of milk in the road and followed the Neighbour.

"We shall have this turnip up in a flash," said the Milkman with great confidence.

But, though he lent all his strength to the pulling, it was of no use. The turnip would not move.

"This is a matter for the whole neighbourhood," said the Milkman. And he ran to call others to their aid.

Now the first he met along the road was the Little Maid returning from her marketing.

The Little Maid dropped her basket and ran to call her brother from the hayfield. The Brother dropped his rake and ran to fetch the Village Dandy.

The Village Dandy dropped
his fine red coat and hastened
to tell his sweetheart. The
Sweetheart dropped her wash
and ran to summon the
Whistling Boy. The Whistling
Boy dropped his fishing rod
and whistled to his dog.

The Dog told the Cat;

and the Cat told the Mouse.

And soon the whole neigh-
bourhood had gathered in the
old Farmer's turnip field.

"How very fortunate we are to have such good friends!" exclaimed the Farmer's Wife.

And they all set to with a will. Forming a long line, and each holding fast to the next, they gave a great shout and a great pull.

With that the earth opened, and up came the mighty turnip with such force that they all fell backwards.

So excited was the old Farmer at seeing its size, that he could find no words to express his thanks to them.

On the day of the awarding, the turnips were brought from miles around to where the Mayor waited in the market place.

There were pink turnips and white turnips, red ones and yellow ones, fat and thin. But though more wonderful turnips had never been seen, the old Farmer's turnip was the largest of them all.

Thus it came about that the happy Farmer became the owner of the beautiful black-spotted cow.

There was much merry-making and celebration in the village, and none were more merry than the Farmer, the Farmer's Wife, the Grandson, and the Granddaughter, the Neighbour, the Milkman, the Little Maid, the Brother, the Village Dandy, the Sweetheart, and the Whistling Boy – to say nothing of the Dog and the Cat and the Mouse.

And never, during the long winter, did the farmer's family or his good neighbours want for food.

There was plenty of good white milk  and thick, rich cream,

fresh golden butter and fine mellow cheese

and turnip enough for all!